HADAD

The Innkeeper's Journey

MAC
McCONNELL

ONE WAY BOOKS

HADAD

ISBN 978-0-9800451-2-3   10 Digit 0-9800451-2-6
Library of Congress Catalog Card Number 2008937721

www.OneWayBookS.org — (954) 680-9095

DEDICATION

I dedicate this book to the loving memory of my brother Merek (1942-2001). He accepted me at face value, that's a true friend.

Two are better than one,

because they have a good return for their work:

If one falls down,

his friend can help him up.

But pity the man who falls

and has no one to help him up!

Eccl 4:9-10

Other Books by Mac McConnell

"I'm pregnant and the child is not yours."
The worst news any bridegroom could receive.
Joseph is an unexpectant father now faced with
decisions that effect all of history.

*What Mac does like no other on stage, he
now does on paper. You feel as if you are
living each scene as Mac unfolds the drama,
beauty and excitement of ancient history.*
Tony Hammon, speaker, author

Why would a nice Jewish boy grow up to be a
despised tax collector in Jericho? Then what
would compel Zacchaeus out on a limb to see
the latest in a long line of *would-be* messiahs?

*The reader plunges into the head and heart of
Zacchaeus and the encounter that changed his
life. I recommend you read and reread this little
volume.*
Terry Whalin - Whalin Literay Agency

A shepherd boy misses the announcement of a
lifetime, angels! Angels have come to tell of the
birth of Messiah in Bethlehem. But Bozra is
asleep on the job. His journey begins, though
time after time he's a day late, until....

*Just as Mac brings characters to life on stage,
he transform the written word into another
another world. You won't want an intermission.*
Janet Folger, president www.F2A.org

What they say about Mac's Books

I bought your book. I read it in one sitting. I couldn't put it down.
I look forward to reading your next.

Lisa Hench.

As I read Mac's first book I found myself laughing out loud and
then warmed to my core at his uncanny ability to draw me into each
character.

Dr. Bob Barnes. Author, speaker,

Almost immediately, I was immersed in the mind of this character.
His inner thoughts were revealed in a kind of poetry Mr. McConnell
used as he wrote this book.

Joe Dunfee

I loved it. A powerful message wrapped up in a delightful story.

Sandi Powell

You will laugh and cry as you identify with the characters in this
powerful journey.

Gigi Graham author/speaker

Mac's dramas are captivating, and his novel kept me turning pages
until I was sorry it ended. Definitely a home run.

Brian Doyle, MVP 1978 World Series

This book touched my heart and made me feel complete. Thank you
for the inspiration!

Fran Napolitano

TABLE OF CONTENTS

Foreword

Prologue

Order Information

FOREWORD

Knock.

Knock.

Will Hadad answer the request? His inn is full of patrons, and paying ones to boot, when a weary traveler arrives late at night, knock—knock. He doesn't need anymore people to care for, or about.

One never knows when a knock at the door catapults life into a new and different direction. Reluctantly, Hadad, a simple barkeep, ushers Joseph and his very pregnant wife to a place of last resort, to sleep with animals in the stable. A baby, born that evening, placed in a borrowed manger, tugs at Hadad's hard heart, and to his surprise he is melted into caring. The child grows and the callous barkeep develops a closeness with the family and especially the precocious little boy. When the family disappears, he longs for his small friend and even after thirty years cannot forget the lad.

Rumors spread of a dynamic man touching and changing lives, loved my many, but hated by more. His name said in whispers—the name of … could it be he?

Hadad has to wonder, "has my little Yeshua grown into a man?"

Once again McConnell takes the reader on a dramatic journey into forgotten history that tingles your heart and shakes your soul. Join Hadad; will he quest for deeper understanding to find the truth?

Will you?

Jodee Kulp, Executive Director,
Better Endings New Beginnings

PROLOGUE

"Take heed, take heed.
Hear this day all who abide in the world of
Caesar Augustus,
the most gracious and righteous Emperor of Rome.
Each one will be inscribed to the census of
His Majesty by province of Herod, your King of
Judea. Make way to the house of your lineage.
All persons in the sound of my voice, Jew or gentile,
slave or free, compliance is decreed this day forth
in the lands and possessions of his royal and
great Caesar."

HADAD

The centurion bellowed the dictate from his stallion from one end of Bethlehem to the other.

"You there, your beer cold?"
"Yes, yes of course." Hadad had no real choice.
"Fill'er up, if you know what's good for you."
"Yes, yes of course." Hadad was glad to see the back end of the horse and the soldier leaving town.

The Roman was as big as his horse and smelled like one too. Soldiers seldom stopped in Bethlehem. They didn't much care for sheep or shepherds and if it weren't for sheep and shepherds there wouldn't be a Bethlehem, and no need for a cozy little inn at the end of town.

Hadad was born here, so he was not going anywhere to be counted. The same for Beatrice, his wife.

It began.
Just a few at first.
The tired two-tiered structure was not the first choice for a discriminating traveler who had the means to insist on finer things. Their prices reflected that. But the rooms were clean and quiet.

Prologue

The noise of the town was distant, and there were fields out back to accommodate many animals. The inn, shabby some said, but Beatrice's cooking rivaled any anywhere. Her honey baked bread made grown men drool without shame.

"We should close this dilapidated inn and open my bakery," she nagged Hadad often, but not any more. She had new things to nag about.
"Dear, have you seen to the latrine."
"Yes, just this morning."
"That's not what I meant."

Hadad knew what she meant. And he knew finally, he could be the one right, this time. The census would bring customers. Perhaps lots of customers.

It could be the best of times.

ONE
The Woman

I thought surely it would be the best of times when
  I met Beatrice.
I could not have imagined these last years when
  I just knew I would lose it all.
Of times a real job sounded real good.
    Times when I couldn't hold my head up
      or begin to pay my debts.
        A failure.
I'll just walk out back of the barn and slit my throat,
  I thought. But that would make a mess and
  Beatrice would expect me to clean it up.

No, truth is, Beatrice never gave up on me. And that
  kept me from disappearing in the night with
  her little sister, who seemed to have a
  considerable interest in me,
and apparently in every other eligible bachelor in
  Bethlehem.

HADAD

Beatrice's "You can do it, Hadad," sounded more
like, "You *will* do it Hadad."
But it had a way of keeping me trying when my
    trying was tried out.
I'm not sure which helped the most, Beatrice's
    nudging, or my fear of failure.

There were many times when the only one sitting
    at my bar was me.
If it weren't for stale beer, there would be no beer.
    That was most depressing.
Beatrice said I couldn't go a day without a drink.
    She could be right.
Why spend a whole day without a beer?

That may have been my first attraction to her.
Her father's never ending supply of beer.
    A most generous man.
So, I was often *in the neighborhood.*
    Every holiday; every occasion.

That's not fair. Beatrice was a beauty.
    A bit aggressive, but a beauty.
Never satisfied to sit quietly and listen to
    man talk.
Never satisfied to retire with the women
    and their chatter.

The Woman

She always had a fresh loaf or cake for me to take
    home.
"Beatrice, no, you will get me fat." I protested,
    slightly.
"Hadad, I love to bake, don't be silly, take it."

She would hand me the warm bundle wrapped in
    white linen that she embroidered.
It was irresistible,
    and Beatrice was too.
She pressed my hand to the loaf.
I savored the heat from the fresh baked bread
    and from her hand.
Then she looked at our hands. She looked up.
    All the time stroking my hand and smiling, a
    little smile with half open dreamy eyes.

She wanted to marry I knew.
I knew?
    The whole town knew.
She was the oldest and her sister was the talk of
    all the mothers.
        Her sister had a host of admirers.
"Too many men hanging around that back porch."
    The rumors spread.

But, my Beatrice had made up her mind, and
    when she makes up her mind
    you might as well fall in line.

I would have chased her sister,
    but she was such a tease, too much work,
    and I could not keep her happy,
        if you know what I mean.

Beatrice thought me handsome.
"That makes two of us," I agreed.
"You two make a beautiful couple," her mother
    liked to remind me.
"You two will make beautiful babies," she would
    add to Beatrice's blush.
The talk of babies meant one thing,
    Beatrice *will* be married.
A girl unmarried by her sixteenth birthday could
    end up doing her sister's laundry.
I could do worse, much worse
    from the looks of this little town.
I certainly could not marry into a shepherd's family.
I could not, would not, do the field work and anyone
who marries a shepherd will be a shepherd.
    These were the choices of Bethlehem.
        That and butcher.

The Woman

We *were* a handsome couple I had to admit.
She received the stares as we walked to market
    during our hastened courtship—Beatrice's
    sixteenth was just two months away.
But I still caught a glimpse or two from the young
    girls, the will-be-weds at any cost.

Now, in only ten years, we both have enjoyed too
    many buns from Beatrice's baking.
We both roll out of bed now,
    and have difficulty passing in the hall.
The hall where we once bumped and bounded
    upstairs in hope of babies.
Now we wait for the other to pass.
    There is no bounding up, or down the stairs.
        And no babies.
Beatrice became detached, discouraged.
    There were whispers she was barren.

"Beatrice, I love you, *you*, you are all I want,"
    I insisted.
"Thank you my dear, but I want to give you a son.
    And I will."

So we tried,
    and tried,
        and tried.

Trying is good.

TWO
The Place

Ethan, Beatrice's father, gave us this old place as a
    wedding gift.
"He just wants it off his hands," she said.
But when Ethan showed us around I was drooling,
    at first.
"At least three acres. A stable to the east. Sits just
    south of the main road with willows on the
    hill behind and a stream to the west. And a well,
    as well, Hadad," he said.
"Beatrice, there's a stable."
"It's a hole in the hill, Hadad."
"It's a cave, Beatrice, and I think that qualifies as a
    stable."
        She seldom saw things the way I do.
"It will need a little fixing up." I was enthusiastic.
        It was either this or work for the butcher and
            smell like a goat.
        To be covered in blood all day was not my
            style.

19

"It will need an overhaul, and who will do that?"
    Beatrice seemed depressed.
    The honeymoon might be over
        before it was over.
"Too many floors, too many rooms," Beatrice
    complained.
"Two floors are not too many." I must admit the
    first look was more appealing than the next.
    I suggested we spend our wedding night
    there.
"No!" She knew something I didn't.

Even I became anxious.
The floors didn't just creak, boards were busted.
The stairs were missing steps and the doors
    were barely propped in the doorjamb.
    I had to hold tight lest they fall to the floor
    when I reached to open them.
One room, upstairs on the right, was well lit,
    but that was from a hole in the roof.
    A flock of pigeons turned it into a guestroom
    and they didn't care for our intrusion.
"You will have to move on," I told them.
"*We* will have to move on,"
    Beatrice assured us all.

The Place

I was about to agree when Ethan showed me this
   side room.
   A parlor I supposed,
     or private sitting room.

"I built it for my mother-in-law, Hadad, but she
   didn't care for it. Said it was the coldest room
   the house," Ethan said with a sneer. "Hadad,
   I was thinking it could make a nice little
   tavern. It has its own entrance.
   Just a thought."

Just a thought?
   A brilliant thought, I thought.
Beatrice thought I lost my mind.
   But I had it made up.
"Course I expect to share the profits," Ethan said.
"Sure, sure, of course," I foamed at the mouth.
   I could see beer foaming over mugs.

I felt the pride of owning a successful inn with
   reservations a year in advance,
     the envy of Judea,
   a dining hall, servants, cooks, *and a tavern*
   which even had its own entrance.
I thought a sign over the door was in order.

"HADAD'S HIDEAWAY"
    has a nice ring to it.
But that might take some convincing.

Enthusiasm was all I needed,
    at first.
Starting out with a roof over my head and a tavern
    downstairs was a dream I had not even dreamt.
I've always wanted to work for myself.
    Not much for taking orders.
"Can I get another beer here?"
    were the only orders I would hear.

The inn needed about everything, but my bar got
    my attention.
Beatrice had the place whitewashed,
    after the roof was patched and the pigeons
    moved on.

Now, listen to this.
I rigged a drain to run under the house from the
    sink.
It was a moment of genius,
    which pales in comparison to what I'm
    about to tell you.

The Place

Beatrice had me carry the provision from market
    to the cellar.
A cold, dark, musty cellar with a mere ladder and
    vermin that scurried for cover when I poked
    the lantern through the hole in the floor.

But now the good part.
I rigged a bucket and rope with a pulley to raise
    and lower the stock.
Even Beatrice thought it was a good idea.
What she didn't know
    what she didn't need to know is
        about my stock.
           My beer and wine.

I knew she would never darken that hole;
    it would be the perfect place to stash my
        stash.
I thought, *how perfect*, when I pulled up my first
    haul from the cellar.
        The wine was cool.
        The beer was cool.
        In the middle of the summer.
    Brilliant.
It cooled my lips. It cooled my mouth, my throat. It
cooled my stomach. It cooled my thoughts.

Genius.
Certainly my customers would agree.

I was destined to be the best barkeep
    in Bethlehem, that was sure.
    I see a bustling business.
    Regulars lined up.
Beatrice caring for the inn,
    and the food,
    and the sheets,
    and the customers,
    and the reservations,
    and the bills.
        Just the basics.

I would surely hire someone to tend our little
    stable.
    We needed the chickens and eggs—cows,
    goats and such, for fresh milk, and meat,
    and butter—for our little dining room and
    overnight guests. I wanted pigs, but Beatrice
    said, "Not on your life."
        I figured that meant no.
We, well she, started a little garden
    which needed constant attention just to keep
    out the varmints,

The Place

the four and two legged kind.
Beatrice had a knack for growing.
    She planted some stupid little
        good-for-nothing flowers.
"They will look wonderful on our tables.
    Our guests will appreciate them."
She was right. But what a waste—to
    pick flowers—stick them in a jar
    just to throw them out in a day or two.
"Feed them to your precious cow, maybe that will
    sweeten her milk."
    I did, and it did,
        I guess.

"Hadad, take out the garbage,
    set the tables,
    weed the garden and
    do something with yourself,
    you look a fright."
    Beatrice's daily chant.
"I must polish the bar,
    and shine the mugs and, and
    fix a leak in the drain."
    My usual response.
"Hadad, that was the same list from yesterday.
    Now please, that can wait.

Besides you look pale spending endless hours behind that bar. It will do you good to get some sun."

Yes, it could wait.
Yes, it was the same list.
An important list.
It's what I wanted, needed to do.
Who needs sun?

THREE
The Business

The only real rush of business was during the
Passover season. Pilgrims from Hebron and
Marisa, even from Ascolon.
Once, a man from Joppa who was apparently lost.
All headed to Jerusalem for the Feast of Unleavened
Bread.
Being on the south of town meant I got first crack,
but one, two weeks a year, are not enough to
pay the bills on this place
much less my fresh beer.
On their way home they pushed straight through.
Not wanting to stop.
Not having any shekels much less denarius
after the high-priced marketplaces of the
holy city. If they did, they bought a loaf of
bread.
That's all.
I tried to tell them, "One loaf, one beer."
Alas, that fell on deaf ears.

Then another year of,
> *Hadad, where are you?*
Another year of,
> *Hadad, take out the garbage.*
And another,
> *set the tables.*
And,
> *do something with yourself,*
> *you look a fright.*
And, *Hadad, you've run off your customers,*
> *what customers you have, with your dumb*
> *stories.*

"They like my dumb stories," I tried to tell her.
> "I mean my stories."
>> Not dumb!
Maybe they were—a little—dumb.

FOUR
The Friend

With luck Jared will be in to complain about
   business and join me for a round. He has a
   couple of rentals that seldom see the face of
   travelers.
When he toured the tavern he became my first
   customer with a tab.
      A tab his wife never knew.
"You should join the guild, Hadad. You will be
   surprised. It will bring you customers,"
   Jared told me often.
He knew everyone in town and beyond.
When I needed something, Jared had the answer.
Not a handsome man. Not a big man.
      But a good friend.
I apologize.
I haven't told you about my friend, Jared.
Nice fellow. Not ambitious, but steady.
      Full of ideas and friend to all.

Quiet man with a wit as dry as dust. If it wasn't for
the fact he couldn't disguise that smirk of his,
he might have lost his friends. So, it was best
to watch Jared to see if he was leading you on.
The kind of man you would ask to stand up for you
at your wedding.
I did.
The kind of friend that would let you barge in and
interrupt him with just about anything.
I would.
The type of man that would give you the clothes
off his back.
I wouldn't.
Jared covered for me. He defended me. He listened.
But he would tell me when I was wrong.
He isn't perfect.

"Herod saw all the people in Jerusalem during the
feasts and no doubt decided he could squeeze
more taxes from his domain with a census,"
Jared said.
"I thought it came from Rome, from Caesar?"
"Same thing."
Jared knew these things. He may not be much for
business, but he knew the business of
Bethlehem and had no patience with
governments.

FIVE
The Census

A big, old centurion brought the decree.
Not a respectable chore for a soldier.
    He looked like he was on his last leg,
      as did the horse he rode in on.
His armor was dinged and chinked.
His sandals cracked and caked with dirt and dung.
The plume long gone out of his helmet.
    Still, his sword gleamed in the sun.
      It alone signaled respect.
      "...Make way to the house of your lineage.
      all persons in the sound of my voice..."
He repeated the census dictate in Greek, Hebrew
 and Latin.
    His Greek and Latin came easy.
      His Hebrew was pitiful.
I remember that soldier.
    He changed my life.

HADAD

I sensed it as he urged his mount on out of town.
I gladly filled his bladder with beer even if
    I had no choice in the matter.
He looked like he could use a cool one.

Then, Decimus, the census man came
    from Cyprus.
        Not an important city.
Of course Bethlehem was not much either, as towns
    go.
"Rome will not hire a census taker from their own
    town. So they pay somebody room and
    board to do a job anyone here can do," Jared
    said with contempt.
"The next thing you know they will charge us to be
    counted," I figured.
"Hadad, don't give them ideas," Jared said. "And,
    who says they won't?"

SIX
The Sheep

Bethlehem was close enough to Jerusalem for the
fringe of latest news and doings from the
Jews and the Romans, and the whims of the
almighty Herod.
Travelers, shepherds mostly, brought tales back
from Jerusalem, or when herding their lambs
to be sold for sacrifice.
That was the real business of Bethlehem.
Lambs.
Spotless.
Holy lambs for slaughter at the
altar of God.
They didn't smell holy to me.
They clogged the streets.
They awakened me at unholy hours with
their bleating and clanging of those bells
hung round their necks.

HADAD

It's a good thing I like lamb stew or I'd of put up a
    roadblock and charged a toll.
But that could divert what little traffic that passed
    by our inn.
        A mistake.

"If it weren't for lambs, there would be no
    Bethlehem," the shepherds reminded.

"Hadad, quit your grumbling and set up the stand
    outside. See if they'll buy some bread."
Might as well.
    Sleep was over when they came through
        before the sun came up.

Hawking bread to shepherds was no dignified job
    for a barkeep such as myself, but my
    regulars would not see what I was doing at
    this hour.
If I had had any customers we'd-of burned the
    midnight oil and solved the world's problems
        long before sunup.

"Bread this morning and beer this night,"
    I chanted to Beatrice's embarrassment.

The Sheep

I got few takers, but someday they would all
remember and come back.
    Someday.
I thought about hiring young girls,
    but that didn't sit well with Beatrice
      to say the least.
She said something about me losing my mind.
Which was what I might do
    if business didn't pick up.

I joined the guild with Jared.
I volunteered for a committee and suggested they
    meet at my place.
This was a good idea, 'cept they didn't think they
    should have to pay for every round.
So, I watered the beer a bit and it all worked out.

"How is it you have the time to work on that dumb
    committee, Hadad?"
"Dumb committee? You wouldn't understand,
    Bea."
    She did, but that was the best I could come
      up with.

SEVEN
The Inn

But that was then; times are changing.
Fresh paint sloshed on old sidings.
    Shutters straightened.
    Gardens tended.
    Streets raked.
    Dung shoveled.
    Roofs fixed.
    Fresh hay gathered.
    Laundry flapping in the wind.
    Houses swept clean.
    New curtains everywhere.
    Even latrines whitewashed.
You'd a thought a god was coming to town.

Our rooms began to rent.
    Customers.
    Tenants.
        Freeloaders.

Our first customers were second cousins of
    Beatrice.
    No deposit.
        Doubtful, even a payment at all.
But a beginning.
    Beatrice was overjoyed to see them and
have them stay,
        at first.
    The man, *useless,* Beatrice endlessly repeated
under her breath.
        At least he made me look ambitious.
The woman thought she was a princess.

Scragglers were next.
Those unable to afford uptown prices.
    Those not here to be counted at all,
        but to see who they could see,
            get what they could get.
They paid in advance.
If they couldn't, "Well, just move on then."
    Many did, out back with their tents or bare
        blankets. Stealing hay from my bales
        to make their beds.
They'd slip back in, cozy up to my bar, or to
    anyone that might buy a round.
I saw them work the crowd.

The Inn

Backslapping, compliments.
    Waiting to order.
        Waiting to catch a free one.
Oh, the stories they told,
    "wife fell off the cart and broke her leg;
    children need a doctor, but we don't
        have...
    we were attacked by bandits and they took
        everything."
Yes, it worked, they caught a few.
    A few too many.
    I dragged them out back.
But they'd be back.
I insisted they see the stream before they see a
    beer.
    Their odors were not appealing, even my
        animals turned to stare.

More and more the town swelled.
    Who knew so many born in Bethlehem?
        The inns filled.
    Who knew so many could return.
        Even the private homes bulged.
I raised my rate.
    Had to.
No sense missing this opportunity.

HADAD

I told Beatrice, "Your cousins need to go."
    "Show them the bill," she said.
    They left in the middle of the night.
        Beatrice didn't mention them again.
I evicted the scragglers for higher class guests.
    Ones that could linger at my bar,
    and buy a round of drinks for the entire
    tavern, or all of Bethlehem.
They had to pass other inns to get to ours,
    but eventually they did.
    First, because we were cheaper.
Then it was for a different reason.
    A very good different reason.
        They discovered Hadad's Hideaway.
And yes, Beatrice's cooking.
I once agreed with Beatrice, there were too many
    rooms in this old place.
    But, not any more.
When "more" came our way they were picky,
    but they could pay,
        and that was fine by me.
    I rose to the occasion.
Beatrice took exception to their demands.
    I took orders.
    Orders for more ale,
        wine,

beer,
    whatever.

"It's not decent to serve drink during daylight,"
    Beatrice announced for any to hear.
"It is not decent to make my customers wait,"
    I reminded at every chance.
"This is what I was born for, Beatrice."
    She huffed
        turning away.

Cool water from our stream chilled the mugs and
    tankards.
        My customers were pleased.
Their order ready before they ordered.
    They were impressed.
Most ran a tab.
    I added a service charge for my trouble.
    They didn't mention it; for their wives might
    find out how much time and denarii they
    spent at the bar.
Besides, would I ever see them again?

Jared came round often to help behind the bar. He
    had his own tenants too.
        I sent him my overflow.
He was a happy man.

Hadad

I didn't water my wine—so much.
The beer was fresh and foaming.
I hired young Abigail to tend the dirty mugs. She
    added a scosh of flavor to the place.
I kept the mugs full.
I even bought on credit with Reuben from
    Bethany, which was smart of him,
    since I had been solicited by
    Sol from Hebron.
Just as I planned,
    our tavern was becoming famous.
        Never a doubt.

I felt like the smartest man in Bethlehem with
    business booming.
We had a waiting list from many who pitched
    their tents in our fields.
They came in to eat or buy Beatrice's bread.
    And quench their thirst.

EIGHT
The Boom

Everyone's business was booming.
    Some were caught off guard, but no
    complaints.
So many people coming and going and staying.
Carts laden with family possessions
    they dared not leave behind.
Carts often broke down. Some fell to pieces
    dragged to the side to be mended. Others,
    left behind, destined to become firewood or
    fence stock.
Even more business to our little town.

I saw it all.
    Worn-out travelers.
    Families wearing old, dusty clothing.
    Shoes and wraps needing attention.
    Streets covered with droppings.
    Dogs barking.

Flies buzzing.
Babies crying.
Men yelling.
Children screaming.
Music to my ears.

Pickpockets roamed through the droves.
 Clever thieves.
 They sent their children to distract
 unsuspecting mothers then pretended
 to fetch them while snatching valuables
 from under their noses.
The market, once sparse with dribs and drabs,
 now bulged;
 customers, merchants,
 strangers, charlatans,
 bargains and fakes.
 Constant cook fires peaked every appetite
  offering charred this or stewed that.
The town bakery was pushed to capacity.
 More orders for Bea.
 Leather workers ran out of supplies.
  Prices went higher.
Peddlers moved goods from one table to the
 next, as if no one noticed.

The Boom

Racks of used clothing were sorted and
    displayed.
Needles and cords busily mended holes and
    tears.
Tent makers patched skins and sold wares.
Gaming tables setup everywhere after dusk.
Loose "ladies" taunting behind transparent
    veils, beckoning with undulations.
Players of tambourines, and flutes, and lyres
    enticed with music.
Thieves pummeled in the market.
    Instant justice for all to see.

We were becoming a city.
    A real city.

NINE
The Manager

"Hadad, where are you?"

Me thinks Beatrice might have a thing or
two for me to do.

"I'm busy."

"With what?"

"I'll be right back." I wouldn't be right back, but it
was the best I could come up with.

I started toward Jared's...

"Hadad! Don't go anywhere. You need to clean the
stable."

"What! Clean the stable? For what?"

"We have travelers with animals."

"So? A stable is a stable. I built the overhang."

"Yes you did, but we need fresh hay, and the stable
must be presentable. We could charge extra
for boarding their animals if the stable looks
like something."

She had a point.

I spent the rest of that day in that stable.
It had been a long time.
    It was disgusting.
    Alright, she had had a good point.

"Where do you want this?"
    The skinny boy startled me.
I turned to see a small wagon with two bales of
    hay stacked high.
"Where do you want this?"
"I heard you. There," I said.
Beatrice never stops.
    But we did need the hay.
After one bale was spread I divided the other.
    Half in the pen.
    The other I dumped in the manger,
        which was a mistake.
It tipped over and one leg broke.
I went to pick it up, but it fell apart in my hands.
    That will have to wait.
"Hadad, don't forget to clean out the manger, and
    fill it with fresh hay."
Perhaps I could do it today after all.
All this fuss with who knows what to expect.
    I needed to get to my bar.
        To do something important.
Anything but stay in this godforsaken stable.

The Manger

The manger was past repair.
I, not the handiest man in town, did not know what
    to do.
We will just have to do without.
    But that wouldn't do with Beatrice.
        Jared will have a solution.

"Jared. Jared. Are you here?"
"Yes, of course my friend. What can I do for you?"
"You can help me find a manger or build one or
    something."
"Hadad, just go to Ira and get a new one."
"I don't need a new one, Jared. I just need one for a
    month or so during the census. Why go to
    the expense of a new one?"
"Where do you think you will find a used manger?
    Nobody gives away used mangers; they use
    them for firewood. Just go see Ira."
"Alright already. See you later then.
    I will see you later?"
"Yes, of course."

Jared was right, I should have thought of that, but
    Ira is expensive. With lots of work no doubt.
        The only carpenter in town.

"Ira, Ira, oh my, you look busy."

"Hadad, I'm swamped. I hope you don't want a
    manger."

"Well, that's exactly what I want, need."

"I have orders coming out of my ears. Everybody's
    in a panic to have their stables and pens
    ready."

"What am I to do?"

"Tell you what. Take that little one there. I made it
    up for Jachin and Birsha."

"They won't need it?"

"Don't know. I told them it was too little in the first
    place. Now they haven't been back. Just
    take it. A loan till I can make you a new one.
    I know it's small, take or leave it. Perhaps you
    could lose my tab at the tavern for awhile."

"Tab? What tab? No hurry on the other then.
    Thanks."

It *will* do just fine. Wait'll I tell Jared.
    A borrowed manger.

Perfect.

TEN
The Plan

The census man, Decimus, was busy,
  but lazy.
He hired help, but that didn't help much.
"The first one's on me," I told him the day he
  arrived.
I knew it would be good to be good to him,
  and it was.
He sent me my first real customer, and came to see
  me that first night.
"I'll run a tab," I told him,
  but I never thought about calling his bill,
I figured he would know everyone that came to
  town in case I needed to know anything.
I treated him like he was somebody.
He came early each evening to make his way to the
  corner, in the back, in the dark, away from
  notice.
Rome was not prepared for so many to be reckoned
  and the lines were backed up all day.

Many protested,
    but this was perfect.
My travelers needed to stay for more than a night
    or two.
    No telling how long.
They drank more than they should.
    Then drank more.
They even bought me drinks.
    I didn't fill my mug.
I kept my wits about me and took it easy
    as Beatrice insisted.
    At least I tried.
Fresh, foaming, cool beer was irresistible.

Beatrice complained about the noise late into the
    night. She was a small town girl.
"What can I do?" I appealed. "I have a reputation
    to consider."
Some from the tents out back had dancing girls.
"Hussies," Beatrice called them.
    "Cheap entertainment," I called them.
They danced for a beer or two, which I seldom
    supplied. Customers bought them all they
    wanted to keep them dancing.

Good thing Beatrice went to bed early.

The Plan

The dancing often got, umm,
    sensational.

People came and went and the loot piled up.
Some couldn't pay—thanks to the census taking
    so long—they paid with donkeys,
        or mules and one droopy old mare.
The stable was full and Beatrice finally agreed, so I
    hired a boy.
"You need to sell some of these raggedy animals,"
    he complained. "I can't take care of them
    all, and this manger is too small. And that
    horse, why do you keep that old horse?"
"Yes, tell you what. You sell 'em and I'll make it
worth your while.
    Just between you and me, understand?"

I knew the census would not last forever, but it
    seemed possible. Decimus was in no hurry.
    His first steady job in years, he admitted.
"Working for the government has its benefits,"
    he told me. "You should consider it, Hadad."
"Enjoy yourself and take it easy, Decimus,"
    I encouraged him, every chance I got.

Hadad

Most didn't like him much.
They blamed him for this mess.
I thanked him.

ELEVEN
The Baby

One night.
Jared passed out. His head on the counter.
    Packed bar.
        Late.
    Decimus snoring in his corner.
Two men complaining about their wives
    and life in general.
A knock.
    I barely heard it.
    Who? At this hour?
For the first time that I could remember I didn't
    want another customer.
I was glad I'd locked the door.
    They will leave.
    Knock, knock. Another knock.
Shhhh, you'll wake Beatrice. She'll expect me upstairs
    I thought out loud, but no one heard me.

I opened the door.

Regretting it wasn't locked.
Anyone else round here would have just
    walked in.
"If you ain't got a reservation, you ain't got a
    room."
Which wasn't exactly true, we had no room if they
    had a reservation, but sounded good.
The man stood there.
"Did you hear me?" I surprised myself,
    so mean—liquor talk.
He then turned away.
Dirty, dragging, pitiful,
    limping, leaning on his staff.
I started to close the door when she groaned.
    I hadn't seen her.
I pushed the door back, and saw a woman.
    Big as a house she was.
    Sitting on a dreary donkey.
She grasped her bulge and lowered her head.

We never had children, but it was obvious
    she was about to give birth,
    right there, sitting on that poor mule,
    or die in the process.
I pulled the door thinking, *Beatrice will hear bout*

The Baby

this and then I will hear bout it.
Confused.
My customers weren't the only ones drinking.
    I was groggy to say the least.
    Why do I have this to deal with now? Can't they
    see we are full? What am I supposed to do?
    Give them our room? Then what, a screaming kid
    in the middle of the night waking my tenants?

She let out such a cry.
    A yell!
    A gasp,
        a moan,
            a sigh.
The man steadied her on the donkey.
"Wait. Just wait." *Why did I say that?*
    I'm just a softhearted barkeep that's all.
I turned, grabbed a lantern, latched the door,
"Follow me."
    I led them round back.
        To the barn.
The man stood in disbelief.
"A stable? A stinking stable? Is this a joke?" he
    asked.
"Any place, Joseph. Any place." She began sliding
    off her mount. He rushed to catch her.

HADAD

"Fresh hay there. Stream that way. G'night."
    A weak thank you was all I got.
    The stable didn't stink all that much,
        to me.
I staggered back to the bar.
    Quiet now.
Two sleeping on the floor. I stepped over, and
    around, and crept upstairs.
They knew the way out.

Sleep came quick.
    Just as quick I awoke.
        To something.
            Out back.
A light.
    Laughter.
        Singing?
I must be dreaming.
    So tired, back to sleep.
    I could regret that.
        All of this.

First thing,
    at least first thing for me, I started to the
    barn.

The Baby

I should take something, a little something,
    I felt guilty.
    I grabbed the teapot still full from last night.
        Fresh bread,
                churned butter
                        and a jar of honey,
                        a perfect offering,
        I felt so kind.
"Morning, Joseph."
I remembered his name. He was poking the small
    fire.
Odd, the ground all around was trodden down.
Looked like an army had been through during the
    night.
"Morning sir," he said.
"Hadad, my name is Hadad, the owner."
"Hadad, come meet my wife, Mary and our
    newborn."
"Newborn?"
"Yes, see, just after you left it began."
The mother, leaning against a hay bale, was indeed
    holding and rocking a baby.
A little baby.
    A beautiful little baby.
I was in a trance.
"Is that for us Mr. Hadad?"

"Huh? Oh yes. Bread, butter and tea. You might
    should put the teapot on the fire. It may be
    cold. And honey. Real good honey."
"Thank you for the wonderful treat." Joseph placed
    everything on a bench and the pot on the
    embers.
"I hope you don't mind, I cleaned out your little
    manger and borrowed it for a crib. I made
    sure your animals had hay."

"You want to hold him Mr. Hadad?" Mary sat up
    and extended the baby to me.
The baby looked surprised.
"Yes," I said without thinking at all.
I stooped, and she handed me this little bundle.
    I was surprised.
        Surprised I liked this so much.
The little he, she, looked right at me, as if to say,
    "Who are you?"
"Yeshua. His name is Yeshua."
    It's a he.
"Yeshua. Good morning Yeshua. Sleep well?"
    That wasn't so brilliant.
But I was holding a baby.
    A beautiful baby.
I think I could have stood there all day.

The Baby

It felt wonderful.
    I felt wonderful.

"Hadad! Where are you?" Guess who?
    Beatrice discovered I was up and out.
        I didn't feel so wonderful.
"I have to go now. Please stay as long as you like.
    Let me know if there is anything you need."
    I turned to leave.
"Hadad."
I turned back. "Yes."
"Should you leave Yeshua with us?"
"Oh. Yes, of course. Sorry. Here. See you soon.
    Let me know if there … you know."

I was not all that anxious to get back to the inn.
I was not anxious to hear what Beatrice had lined
    up for the day.
But I was anxious to tell her about this family.
    About the baby.
        The beautiful boy.
I wanted to suggest we should try having a baby
    again, a son.
I wanted to tell her everything,
    but then I remembered I hadn't told her
        anything.

Beatrice will want to know where I've been.
> She will want to know about this couple in
> > our barn.
> She will want to know what I charged them.
> She will want to know…

"Hadad, where is the bread I baked last night?"
> She will want to know where the bread is
> > she baked last night.

"Bread? What bread?"

"You know what bread."

"Oh, yes, that bread."

"Well?"

"I gave it to the nice couple staying in our barn."

"Couple? Barn?"

"Yes. Beatrice, this nice couple came late last
> night. They needed a place to stay. She was
> pregnant, so I made room in the barn."

"Pregnant, did you say she's pregnant? Poor girl, I'd
> better go see how … ."

"Was, I said *was* pregnant. Beatrice, it happened
> last night. Right in our barn. You should see
> this baby, this boy. It is the most beautiful.
> > Beatrice we should have a child,
> > a boy, try again to have a family."

"Not today Hadad. I have work to do.
> You have work to do.

The Baby

Have you set the table,
    taken out the garbage?
      And Hadad, do something
      with yourself, you look a fright."

So much for excitement.

TWELVE
The Uncle

I started to the dining room,
> but detoured to Jared's
>> to tell him about it all.

Hoping he made it home in one piece last night.

He wasn't that excited until I suggested he rent
> them a cottage.

"Jared, give them a good price. They're special.
> You hear me?"

"Special?"

"Just take care of them, Jared."

"Yes, yes of course. And perfect timing too, a
> tenant moved yesterday."

I helped Joseph with his packs and donkey.
> I had hay delivered.
>> I suggested they keep the little manger—I
>> could get a new one—I didn't even gag on
>> the thought.

Beatrice needn't know.

HADAD

I made sure Jared was fair.
I told him I would stand for his deposit.
    That made Jared gawk.

I visited the little family at least once a day.
    "Did you need anything?" I asked each time.
I even joined them at temple when they returned
    from Jerusalem after Yeshua's circumcision.
I didn't understand why they went there for that,
    but they did.
I hadn't been to temple since, *well a long time,*
    but I didn't mention that.
They liked going. Every Shabbat.
    Beatrice was stunned when I started
    attending.
"You can go," I said.
"And sit in the balcony with the old women? No
    thank you very much."
She seemed skeptical of my new religiousness.
"I see you're still getting your customers drunk."
    She might consider me a bit of a hypocrite.

Yeshua grew. He played with children in his
    neighborhood.
He was always respectful to me.
    I think he liked me.

The Uncle

"Uncle Hadad."

My heart went mush when he called me
"uncle" at barely one.

He looked me right in the face.

He tugged on my beard and patted it into place.

His smile seemed, um, like he knew something.

His eyes twinkled.

Deep and clear.

Childish but ancient.

His curly hair spilled in his face.

His hands often dirty with constant discoveries.

He was into everything, so curious.

He enjoyed pouncing on my belly to make me
belch.

He thought that amusing.

He'd sit on my stomach, put his hands on my
cheeks,

"Oh, Uncle Hadad," he whispered.

I closed my eyes and he pounded my stomach,

"Uncle Hadad!" he shouted and giggled when I
pretended to wake up.

I would do anything just to hear him call my name.

I would have moved next door.

I bought and brought things.

His first dreidl.

His first stick and hoop.

His first tambourine.

HADAD

No doubt his only tambourine.
Mary did not appreciate the tambourine,
     but Yeshua did.

I brought things to Joseph and Mary too.
I wanted them to feel at home—to never move
     and take Yeshua.

Beatrice did not get pregnant and
     we stopped trying, again,
          if you know what I mean.
So I'd see that Yeshua had everything he needed.
"Hadad, you don't have to bring us anything,"
     Joseph told me repeatedly.
"I want to."
As soon as I said it, I knew it was true.
     My selfish side had vanished.
I just thought of them and ordered hay for their
     donkey.
     Brought hot bread.
          Sometimes I sent them a skin of wine.
               I charged the wine to my tavern.
                    No one knew.

Joseph was a hard-working carpenter I'd never
     seen the likes of.
Right away he had work he scarcely kept up with.

The Uncle

But each task was a work of art.
Shavings and scraps of wood heaped up.
    I could watch him for hours.
Yeshua, covered in sawdust, ran to me. He'd sit
    and mimic how I sat with my head propped
    in my hand, or with my arms crossed.
He grunted when I did, belched when I did, and
    laughed so hard his eyes shut as he threw
    back his head.
Joseph would look down his considerable nose
    at us both, and Yeshua and I laughed
    until his father did too.
Mary brought cool water and pomegranate slices.
    I was family.
"Hadad, I want to make something for you to
    remember us by," Joseph said one day.
"But, you are not going anywhere. Are you?"
"Well someday. We need to get back to Nazareth,
    Hadad."
"Oh, of course. I hadn't thought about that."
    I hadn't,
        but of course they would someday.
"How about a manger. Yours is a little small."
"No, no I ordered one from Ira."
"Maybe a table, a desk, a … ."
"I need shelves behind my bar."
"Well maybe something else, you think about it."

At first Ira was glad there was someone else
     in town to relieve the strain and complaints of
     undelivered orders. Then he was jealous,
     everyone was talking about the new
     craftsman, his new competition.
I bought a fine stack of wood. Cedar from Lebanon,
Ira told me so, and was glad now for the business.
"What are you going to do with that?" Jared said.
"Joseph wants to make me something.
     To remember him by."
Now Ira wasn't so glad to see me.
"What about the manger I lent you?
     Did you forget about that?"
"What about the bar tab, did you … ?"
"Say hello *and goodbye* to Joseph for me Hadad."
Ira turned away and mumbled something
     and went to banging on some project.

I didn't know what to ask Joseph to make,
but I would come up with something.
     It would have a place of honor.
          Even Jared would be jealous.

"Fine wood Hadad. What shall I make?"
"I just need to leave it here for now,
     I'll have to let you know."

Then it happened.
Unbelievable.
      So unbelievable, you won't believe what I
            am going to tell you.
      I have trouble believing it myself after so
            long.
      After everything else that has happened.
But when I allow myself to think on it, to tell it,
      it is as real as if yesterday.
Here now, let me get started;
      if I can do it any justice at all.
I was headed to see them.
      To see Yeshua.
I had fresh bread.
I had honey.
      I had to see them today.
But when I turned to Jared's I stopped in my tracks.
I looked around to see who else saw this,
      but everyone was at Jared's.

Now I could see why.
Royalty was there.
That's what it looked like.
I had to stop again and again to take it all in.
To make sure I was seeing what I was
seeing.
Camels with colored blankets, studded harnesses
and, and gold adornments.
Barefoot servant boys with head wraps running here
and there to hold the camels and donkeys
with carts piled high.
I don't know what all.
Children scurried to the servants who handed
them something in little pouches.
They looked amazed.
Then out they came from Jared's cottage.
Kings I guess.
A fat one, a tall one, a dark one.
A sweaty one.
Sweltering in those robes and turbans
and curly toed shoes.
How did they all fit in Joseph's little home?
Then came Mary, and Yeshua atop Joseph's
shoulders waving to the kings.
"Uncle Hadad. Uncle Hadad, come see, come see."
The royalty mounted the camels. Servants climbed

in the wagons and carts prepared to leave.
Children ran dancing and giggling and
making a nuisance of themselves—very
nearly getting stomped.
I could barely breathe.

Joseph swung Yeshua down and he ran inside.
"Look Uncle Hadad, they brought gifts"
"I, I see. Lots of gifts."
    More than I could imagine.
        Beautiful scented boxes.
            Ornate oil jars,
                leather money bags.

What *was* this?

Why would royalty come to the little town
    of Bethlehem?
    To see Yeshua?
"Joseph, do you have plans for keeping all this safe?
    If word of this … ." I knew if word of this got
    out, and it would, there would be demands
    and they could be in danger,
    thieves, bandits, charlatans,
        relatives.

"Hadad," Joseph said. "We didn't expect all this.

We will have to think of something. You're
    right, thank you."
"Joseph, there is a fortune here. You could live on
    this for, I don't know how long."
"Yes, yes, I suppose you're right, but I have so
    much work for such nice customers. So that
    will keep me busy."
"Hadad, is that for us?"
    "Oh, yes, of course."
        I forgot about *my* gifts.
        They seemed so little.

Rushing home,
"Beatrice, you must come this time. There were
    kings and camels and gifts and … ."
"Not today Hadad, I have work to do. You have
    work … ."
"Alright, already I hear you."
    So much for excitement.

I went to temple that Shabbat.
    All of Joseph's neighbors were there.
        Most of the town was there.
        They surrounded him most of the
        time now.

The Visit

Which I didn't appreciate at all,
    thank you very much.
Did I mention the priest?
    They were more than friendly this morning.
    To Joseph I mean.
        Not so much to me,
            if they knew I was there at all.
Everyone watched.
    Joseph made his tithe.
    He had Yeshua by the hand.
        Mary was in the balcony.
The noise was unmistakable.
    It was a large contribution.
    The attention embarrassed Joseph.
Then I saw it.
    A beautiful cabinet.
        On the Eastern wall,
            the one closest to Jerusalem.
        Shining wood, polished, intricate.
    It had Joseph's touch.
He had made a temple gift I bet. One that he
    must've been working on for some time.
Soon I found he made lots of gifts.

He hadn't charged anyone for anything that I heard
    of since those royals came bearing gifts.

I was amazed.
    That is not good business.
        Why?

"Joseph, aren't you collecting for your fine work?"
"I have all I need. Like you, many have been
    generous to me and my family. We want for
    nothing. The Lord provides. Perhaps we can
    be a blessing to others as we have been
    blessed."

"Oh, sure, I see."
    Only I really didn't.

FOURTEEN
The Thunder

I had taken out the garbage.
   The trash mound stunk.
I began to set the breakfast table
   without being reminded.

Everything had finally settled from the census.
Only two tenants remained.
   A few stragglers now and then.
Decimus took up permanent residence.
   A regular boarder was nice.
But it had been nearly two years and the census was
   all but over, 'cept it seemed Rome liked
   having an outpost here, or Decimus simply
   created job security, his government
   retirement.

HADAD

The thunder was a shock.
  A good shock I thought.
Everything was parched
  which kept the men thirsty.
    That was good for business.
The roads desperately need a dousing.
The dust behind each cart looked like a sandstorm,
  and left us short of breath.
Our cow quit giving milk.
  Our stream, a trickle.
  Our well water, muddy.
Opening the door felt like opening Beatrice's oven.
  She even drank a cool one now and then.
"Hadad, I can't even hang the sheets out, the dust
  has them filthy in no time."
A *real* worry,
  our cellar was warming.

But there was not a cloud in the sky,
  and the thunder wasn't a coming rain.
    Not thunder at all.
  That became increasingly obvious.

It was like a stampede.
The ground trembled, and I could not imagine
  what was next.
We were a peaceful town.

The Thunder

Sheep and lambs,
  a caravan at times.
    That's all.

I stood on the front stoop.
A dust cloud loomed up and out from the north of
    town.
The rumble of horses' hooves was unmistakable.
  The churning in my stomach was undeniable,
      made me shudder.
I thought the worse,
  but nothing prepared me for what was
      coming.
I knew it was Rome bearing down, it must be,
  but why?
Men ran into the street to see.
  I waited.
  I walked to the street too.
  I wondered if the children should be outside.

What had Herod so worked up?
I only hoped they were passing through.
  To Hebron. To Marisa.
  To Egypt for all I care.
That must be it.
No reason to stop here

'cept for a cool beer.
    I wouldn't mind that.
But the dark cloud looked indignant, enraged
    like the wrath of god.

"Hadad, what are you doing?
    Where are you going?"
"Not now Beatrice,"
    was all I could think.
My neighbors stopped.
    All looking at the mountain of dust pushing
    forward, swelling up, blocking the sun.
Rays of light piercing the cloud like spears.
    Mothers fetched their children home.
    Men creeping back to take shelter.
Then the noise faded
    to nothing.
    Gloom filled my mind as the cloud
        suffocated the air.
I gasped just looking at it.
My stomach lurched.
I hoped for relief.
    If they stopped, they had business here,
    in Bethlehem.
        Ugly business,
        perhaps horrible, ugly business.

The Thunder

"What is it Hadad?" It was Jared.
"Trouble. It's big trouble, Jared."
"What should we do?"
"Pray."
 "Jared, let's go inside."
"No, I'd best get home."

I sat and waited.
    Wondered.
    Worried.

I heard the screams from town and retreated to
    my porch.

Out of the dust they emerged.
Ten or twelve galloped past and I hoped they were
    going on.
    But they stopped, lined up, to block the way
        to Hebron,
        the way out of town.
        We were trapped.
            No escape.
I didn't know where the rest were.
    I could only imagine.
I stepped behind the door and pulled it nearly closed,
peering back through the crack.

I waited.
> And waited.

My heart stopped as screams saturated the air and
my head.

They came.
> So many.

Hot horses stomped and snorted, yielding to the
riders' commands.

They were drenched.
> Sweat.
>> No! Bloody sweat—filthy sweat.
>>> The soldiers too.

Their swords dripped blood.
> All I could think, this is the end.

Herod was mad, and ruthless, and jealous, and
wouldn't stop until he gained complete
dominion over this land. He must have dreamt
that Bethlehem Jews were a threat of some
kind and decided to kill us all.

Here it comes.
> Soldiers swung their legs hitting the ground
hard, ready to attack.

I latched the door, stepping back wondering how
long before they bust it down to slit my throat.

The Thunder

I snuffed the lantern I forgot and left burning
this morning.
It didn't matter.
I stared at the door.
My breath shallow, quick.
The end was here.
The noise.
The screams.
The horror.
Beatrice!
I started upstairs.
But I heard a mother's cries.
I forced myself back to look out the peephole.
It was even more confounding.
My head was spinning.
The soldiers passed men and women, and…
dare I say…
Who would believe me?
They were killing babies.
Just the babies. Moving from house to house.
They even passed older children.
One man tried to stop a soldier but got the blade,
backhanded as if a trifle. The soldier kicked
him out of the way. Blood splattered.
The man clutched the gash, moaned,
rolled in the dirt, and collapsed.
Why babies?

I started back up the stairs when the back door
    slammed and Lydia screamed.
She was running right at me,
    at the front door.
Lydia, our neighbor,
    Bea's best friend.
        She clutched her baby.
    That little baby that kept us up all night.
        Every night.
That little screamer that I wanted to…
"Move!" she shouted. "Move."
    I did, and Lydia tore by me and out of the door,
    pulling it behind.
        Then the soldier.
I did not try to stop him.
    I knew better.
The smell of death surrounded him.
He slammed me into the wall with a sweep of his
    fist.
I barely survived being crushed by the door he slung
    out of his way.
I saw the blood on my sleeve and
    suddenly felt ashamed.
I burst out the door in chase.
    Not thinking.
    Save Lydia.
    The baby.

The Thunder

Too late.

He caught Lydia, spun her around,
    and stabbed the baby in one motion.
        He may have killed Lydia too.
She collapsed and rolled in the dirt on top of the
    child and wailed, "WHY, WHY?"
I lost control; lowered my shoulder and slammed
    the soldier.
"Why?" I asked.
He elbowed me and grinned.
If he was surprised, he didn't show it.
    Then he stuck his foot into my gut and
        shoved.
"Ask Herod. His orders."
I fell back on Lydia.
    "WHY, WHY, WHY?" she screamed.
    I covered my ears.
I vomited and didn't care.

I helped her to her feet
    and dragged her
    to the inn.

    Blood everywhere.
        Life had stopped.

Lydia pressed her baby to her body.
    She would have smothered it if it weren't
        already dead.
"Beatrice," I yelled. "Beatrice, help."
Beatrice crept out of the door.
    She must've seen the whole thing.

"Yeshua!"

Oh my god, what about Yeshua?

    "Beatrice, I have to go."

FIFTEEN
The Hope

What was wrong with me?
> I forgot. Yeshua is just a little boy.
> The same age as Lydia's baby.
> The same age as all these dead.

I started running to Jared's passing the horror.
> Fear burning in my throat.
>> The soldiers would be there.
>> Nothing short of a miracle could
>> save Yeshua.

Should I be so selfish as to pray for a miracle?
> What sort of a miracle could I hope for?

What would I do without Yeshua in my life?

The biggest soldier I'd ever seen stood at their
> door.

He drug his arm across his face.
> Both covered with blood and filth.

He looked at me.

There was no emotion.

Another soldier brought his horse. He mounted and they left.

When Jared came to the door I sank to my knees. Hope drained away.

"Jared, where are Joseph and Mary, and, and my little Yeshua?"

There was nothing I could do. Maybe there was something I could say.

"Hadad, they are not here."

Was that good news or not?

"Where are they Jared? Where did they go?"

I leaped to my feet.

"I, I don't know." Jared swiped at the blood that leaked from the corner of his mouth. "They must have left in the middle of the night."

Jared's hand was shaking.

A cloth in his hand was shaking.

"They left this. 'Sorry Jared, but we have an emergency and had to leave. Here is money for rent through the end of the month. Please thank Hadad for me, and you too. May God return to you the kindness you have shown us all.'

It is signed, Joseph, Mary, and Yeshua the blessed

one."
"The blessed one? Jared, what does that mean?"
"How should I know?"
"Well, they are blessed if they escaped this."

I saw the stack of wood at the rear door still tied
    together.
There was something written on it too.
    It just said "Hadad's."
Then I saw the drawing.
    A child's drawing.
    It looked like an old tree.
    An olive tree drawn on a corner of the top
    board.
I gathered it all up and drank in the scent of cedar.
    My tears dripped on the drawing.
        I wiped them away.
    That smeared the drawing.
        A little.
I left amazed and confused.
    I thought, hoped, for a miracle.
        I felt selfish.
I couldn't help but wonder, if they were warned,
    why not the whole town?
    At least the families of all the babies.
    The dead babies. How many are dead?

How many towns have the soldiers
    destroyed?
But the soldiers turned back the same way they'd
    come. The ones that blocked the road to
    Hebron joined the killers headed north.
Just Bethlehem?
    Why Bethlehem?
        I must wake from this nightmare.
I went back to the inn.
    Families devastated.
    Blank stares.
    Quiet.
    Stunned.
    Wandering.
    Death.
    Death.
        Dead.
Wailing from inside houses.
I tried not to look.
    Mothers held the death in their arms.
        Others with stomachs slashed lay still.
    Where are the priests?
Where is God?
Is there a god?
    Not here.
    Not today,
        I was sure.

The Hope

Yet, Yeshua was spared.
A miracle?
I set the stack of wood behind the bar,
    then changed my mind and took it to the barn,
    then changed my mind and took it to the
    cellar and then went to feed the animals.
To do something.

Beatrice and Lydia were out back.
    Lydia was digging,
        to bury her baby.
Beatrice held the lifeless body.

"Beatrice, is tomorrow Shabbat?"
    Beatrice glared.
When I started back to temple with Joseph and
    Mary and Yeshua, Beatrice suspected my
    newfound religion was only skin deep.
        Today I wondered
            if it was even that much.

Two mounted soldiers passed. One last sweep.
    I stood.
"Hadad, no," Beatrice insisted.
She grabbed my hand or I would've gotten myself
    killed.

How could they do this and feel nothing?
    My chest ached.
    No more trips to see Yeshua.
    No more talks with Joseph and Mary.
    No more games with Yeshua.
    No more thinking there is something special
        about this family, this child.

But was that fair?
They survived.
    I hoped.
        Hope.
    Would I have any hope now?
    Would anyone?

SIXTEEN
The Storm

Thunder, again.
    My heart rattled—my body shook.
This time it was a storm.
Dark clouds dropped torrents of rain.
We sat as the drops splattered the dirt and our
    clothes.
I looked up.
    Rain splashed my face.
I looked to the street.
    Many sat soaked.
There could never be enough water to wash away
    the blood,
        the hurt,
            the horror
Would the horror ever leave?

The skies darkened.
    I was numb.

Hadad

Did God turn his back on this town, our lives and
all this death?
Was this God at all?
Would I ever see Yeshua again?
Will he remember me?

I was drenched.
Channels of water and blood careened through the
dirt.
Our stream filled with blood.
Thunder.
Lightning.
A deluge.
I longed to be washed away.

SEVENTEEN
The Fear

One week,
  two.
No soldiers but the fear remained.
A family from Hebron passed through with a little
    boy crying—no more than a year old.
His crying taunted us,
    a cruel reminder.

I resented the baby and the family.
    Beatrice scolded me.

"Jared, did you hear the boy crying?"
"Everyone heard it."
He didn't look.
    Who could look?

Soon we could only think that our little town, our

families were going to grow old and die out
without our male children.
If we, if anyone gave birth to a boy…
we had no baby boys at all.
Murdered.
Many of the girls too.
And parents, so many men.
Fathers fighting for their children.
No future.
Was life worth living?
It was useless.
Even without children of my own, the pain
staggered me.
Since the day I held little Yeshua in my arms
I wanted a son.
Who am I to have a son when all these mothers
and fathers lost their heirs, their hope,
their reason for living?
A male child is the pride of any family.

What did we do to deserve this?
I asked everyone,
"What did we do to deserve this?"
The rabbi disappeared.
I wanted to ask him too.
Shouldn't he know?

The Fear

No news.
No one from Jerusalem.
No one from Bethany.
No one from East or North came to Bethlehem.
    We were being avoided.
    Shunned.

One morning, we woke to a baby's cry. I sat up.
    My heart sank.
"Beatrice. Beatrice, did you hear?"
"Yes, is that a baby?"
"Must be."
"Hadad, will the army come again?"

EIGHTEEN
The News

I expected the worse at every event.
    At each new birth.
    At each soldier that came and went.
    At the very sound of thunder I flinched.

Children played—not knowing—their lives—how
    fragile—how short?
Every parent hovered over their little ones.
    Some disguised their boys or kept them
    inside day after day. Circumcisions were rare.
    Joy was awkward. Some left town in
    the night—just disappeared without a word.

Years passed and the nightmares faded.

At times I wondered if it ever happened.
    I spoke of it no more.
        No one did.
        A sacred silence.

I helped build the new synagogue.
    Most of the town did, even shepherds
    joined in.
But I could not think about attending.
    Until…
"Hadad."
"Yes, Beatrice. I set the table."
"No, not that. Hadad, I have news. Yeshua."
"Beatrice, there are many with that name."
"Come, listen to what Lydia told me."
"I must take out the garbage and do something with
    myself."
"Ha-ha Hadad. Listen. I think you will want to hear
    this.
    The butcher told Ira,
        who told Sol,
            who told Lydia … ."
"Ummm, Beatrice that's a lot of who-tolds.
    You know I don't care for third-hand tolds."
"Since when? Shush. Believe what you want.
    The word is that a man named Yeshua was

in Jerusalem."

"Like I said, there are lots of Yeshuas, especially in
that city. What's news about that?"

"Have you talked to Jared? He heard too. Everyone
that was in temple yesterday heard it."

Temple.

I regretted not going. Not since … .

"What did everyone hear?"

"The man Yeshua started a riot in the temple."

"A riot? How? What about?"

"Lydia said, they said, he was furious at the money
changers and the merchants. He called them
thieves and started a riot and a stampede."

"A stampede? You are not making sense. I'd better
go talk to Jared."

"Yes, do. And, ask him about the miracles."

"Miracles?"

"Go."

I did. My head spun.

What to think? What to believe?

Lydia I wasn't too sure about.

Jared, maybe Jared.

Why hasn't he said anything?

"Jared, do you have something to tell me?"

"Now, Hadad, don't get all worked up."

"Worked up? Beatrice told me you were at temple
and heard about Yeshua. Why haven't you
said anything?"

"You won't listen to anything I tell you about
temple. You're mad at God, remember?
Why would I tell you about this?"

"Yeshua!"

"You're right. Yes, yes, I should have told you."

"So, tell."

"Alright, already. Sit. Let me get you some cool
water and I'll tell you everything."

"You'd better."

He did.

Slowly.

Too slowly.

The more I heard, the more I wondered. It had been
some thirty years. Maybe more.

Jared said the priests were frantic.

He said the priests called Yeshua a rebel.

He said, they said, the man Yeshua caused
such a ruckus that everyone left the market.

He said, the priests said, Yeshua cursed the

temple and Moses.

"Jared, what did they do to him? Did they arrest him? Is he in jail?"

"I don't think so or they would not have told us this in the first place. They spit and kicked up dust and shook their fist. They just about caused a riot themselves. It appeared, to me, they wanted to get us riled up."

"I should have been there."

"Well maybe not, Hadad. It was so crowded and hot. We were squeezed elbow to elbow like sheep at market. You would have hated it."

"Jared, what about, did you hear about any miracles?"

"Miracles? Didn't hear about any miracles. I thought it a miracle I got out of the temple in one piece. Everyone started shoving, and ranting, and raving, and I don't know what all."

"I can't believe our priest stirred up everyone. Who would imagine our feeble little priest...?"

"It wasn't our priest."

"What? Not ours? Who Jared?"

"They were strangers, but our rabbi treated them like high priests. They were in charge of everything, and made sure everyone knew it."

"Jared, why did they say all this? What was the
    reason they came in the first place?"
"If you ask me, I think they were afraid of Yeshua
    and wanted us to be too."
"Jared, Jared, they must think he is coming here.
    To our town"
"I didn't even think of that. What if he does?"

I thought of it and that thought had me excited for
    the first time in years.

Beatrice wanted to know everything. Then she
asked about the miracles.
"You tell me, Bea. Jared knew nothing."
"What? Oh that's right, it was Bozra."
"Bozra? That shepherd?"
"Yes, Lydia said he stopped at the butcher's and she
    overheard him telling about the man Yeshua
    healing, a blind man I think it was, in
    Jerusalem, after the riot."

"After the riot? Beatrice this is too much. I need to
    talk to Bozra. You say he saw it?"
"I'm not sure. I asked Lydia, but she said he was
    pretty excited and in a hurry to get to the
    fields."

The News

"I better go ask him myself."

"You? You in the fields?"

"It's possible."

"Hadad, he could be a long way from here—out in
one of the north pastures by now. Maybe he
will be back soon and you could see him
then."

I should have gone, but she had a point.
The fields were not my favorite place.
This could be any Yeshua, I kept telling myself.
Or could it?

NINETEEN
The Report

The inn was once again bustling.
Tourists returning early from the Feast,
My tavern has a reputation nowadays.
Many were talking about the riot.
    Many were talking about miracles.
One man reported, "Oh yes, I was there. A cripple
    healed. I saw it alright. But barely, nearly
    missed it. It happened so quick. The man
    jumped up and ran to the temple to show the
    priests. But the priests said it was trickery.
    They warned everyone to ignore this
    Yeshua. 'Steer clear of him or be barred
    from the temple,' they barked."
"The priests must be right then. Why would they
    not want a man doing miracles?" I asked.
"If I was crippled, I wouldn't care about temple or
    priests," someone said.
"Excuse me, I heard it was a blind man,"
    another said.

"No, no, no, it was just a man with a shriveled hand,
   that's all," still another said.

"You sure it wasn't a wild man, possessed? That's
   what I heard," and another said, propped up on
   his elbow from the end of the bar.

"I heard it was Hadad. Yeshua made him handsome."
   A roar from the bunch as they clinked their
   mugs. "But I see it didn't take. Too bad, now that
   would be a miracle." Another roar.

"I don't think that's anything to laugh about, thank
   you very much," I said choking a chuckle.

"Perhaps we should get Beatrice's opinion."

"Fine with me," I offered. I knew she wouldn't be
   down. "But first, who bought that last
   round?"

Others at the bar had this or that to say. One
   outdoing the other. It would be a long night.

I tried to be indifferent.

      They had been drinking, after all.

But I was more than interested.

      What if this Yeshua was the same born not
      twenty paces from where I stand?
      Should I just go to the city and see for
      myself?

"Is this Yeshua still in Jerusalem?" I asked, not really
   looking at anyone.

The Report

Not sounding all that curious.
I wondered, if this is the same Yeshua, the one
they tried to kill—I froze at the thought.
Could it be?
Was it only him they were trying to
kill that day.
No! Impossible.
Hundreds of babies,
just to kill one?
"Don't know where he is." A man at the end of the
counter. "But he scares the you-know-what outa
me. He's possessed if you ask me."
"Possessed? How could a man possessed do such a
wonder?" I asked, a little meekly.
"Who says this is a work of God?" Another.
"There is no other possibility, if it was a miracle?"
Still another.

"If," many agreed.

TWENTY
The Fragment

Jared entered and ordered a beer.

"Hadad, look, look at this," he stammered.

He handed me a torn parchment.

"What? Where did you get this? Is this what I think it is?"

"Yes, a Torah fragment."

"Why? How do you get this?"

"I was at the dump and there it was. The priest must have replaced it and threw it in the dump."

"But it should be burned."

"This one is only scorched. Read it."

"Not now, can't you see I'm busy."

"You will want to read it. It's the prophet Micah."

"Later Jared. Maybe later. What do you know about prophets?" I was too busy listening to the chatter.

They were getting loud and each one trying to get attention as each story grew.

When the last left, I looked at the mess and
    debated, *now or later*?
I decided to clean just the bar
    when I saw it.
Jared left it.
    I tried to ignore it.
    It was just a fragment. *Who is Micah, anyway?*
        What could be so important?

I remembered Jared trembling.
I remembered, I turned away, and back, and he was
    gone.
He never left a drop of beer behind before.

The scrap of parchment looked ready for the dump.
    Burnt edges.
    Something crusty stuck to it.
    Creased. Torn. Crushed.
        Calling.
The last thing I wanted to do was read whatever was
    there. Reading Torah was a distant memory.
        I tried temple.
        If only to be close to Joseph and Mary and
        Yeshua. They were faithful and reverent
        and seem to put such stock in such things.

The Fragment

But all I could see there now was an angry god.
    A bitter god.
    Or no god.

I set the parchment back on the counter and cleaned
    a little more.
I gave in.
    It smelled of refuse.
        Of course.

> WILL STRIKE THE JUDGE OF ISRAEL WITH A
> ROD ON THE CHEEK.
> "HEAR YOU, EPHRATHAH OF BETHLEHEM EVEN
> YOU. YOU ARE LESS AMONG THE THOUSANDS
> OF JUDAH, YET OUT OF YOU SHALL COME
> FORTH TO ME THE ONE TO BE RULER IN ISRAEL,
> WHOSE GOINGS FORTH ARE FROM OF OLD,
> FROM EVERLAST¹

I took out the garbage.
I read it again.
I wiped the counter.
I went to bed.
I slept,
    some.

"Well, did you read it?" Jared was back.

"Yes."

"So?"

"So."

"So, it says out of Bethlehem will come our hope."

"It does?"

"Hadad, what is the matter with you?"

"Jared, what is the matter with you? You got that from the dump. Put it back. Take it from here. It's just . . . ."

"But I just knew you would be overjoyed, at least happy."

"I don't know what to believe anymore. And this could be dangerous. He is dangerous."

"Hadad, here's our hope. You know this man. Born in your stable. Your stable could be famous. Remember you said something about a god coming to town? You should think about a sign."

"You said the priest warned that having something to do with this Yeshua could get you thrown out of the temple, and maybe in jail."

"Hadad, you can't get thrown from the temple you don't go to," Jared snatched the parchment and left.

Famous? I never thought of that.

A sign? Maybe.

TWENTY ONE
The Wait

Yeshua did not come to Bethlehem that year.
But more stories and rumors did.

Lydia and Beatrice were talking one day.
 "...raised him from the dead."
 "Who raised who from the dead?" I blurted.
"Hadad? You listening?"
"Who raised who from the dead? What are you
    talking about?"
"It's true, Leah's cousin from Bethany told her.
    Yeshua raised Lazarus from the dead.
    Everyone in Bethany saw it. Lazarus is famous.
    Bethany is too."

"I better go and see for myself. This is
    unbelievable."
"Hadad, you might want to wait. The priest are
making trouble over this. They could call in
the guards, all the people are following Yeshua."

Beatrice seemed scared.

"I should go."

"If Yeshua goes to Bethany, surely he will come here too. Why don't you make that sign you have been talking about?" Beatrice *was* scared.

Since that day of terror we understood fear.

I wondered about the sign.

Would I be asking for trouble?

TWENTY TWO
The Wondering

Another year—no Yeshua.
    Not to Bethlehem.
        Not to the stable where he was born.
        Not to Jared's.
    Only as close as Bethany for all I know.

I wondered if he remembered me.
    If he was the one.
    Does it matter?
    I wondered if what I believed made any
    difference.
If any of it made any difference.

I will ask Jared for the parchment again. I will hang
    on to it this time.

I never got to tell Yeshua how much I liked him.
How much I missed him.

That I was proud of him.

Passover and busy again. Many headed to Jerusalem
for the Feast.
Many admitted they wanted to see Yeshua.
"I should go, Beatrice. We should go."
"With a full house and a full bar? Not on your
life."

Then it was too late.
People returned on their way home again.
They stopped by my tavern.
One last watering hole before their long trip
home.
They stopped to talk about Jerusalem,
and Yeshua,
and the crucifixions.
Crucifixions?
That happens all the time, but nobody talks
about it.
What? Did I hear that right?
They said Yeshua was crucified.
That he was dead.

The Wondering

That the holy city was filled with fear, and anger,
   and soldiers everywhere.
   I listened. I wondered.
   No one said much more about it.
      Was it over?
         I felt a strange relief.
   Could I get on with my life?

But if Yeshua is dead, does that mean the death of
   miracles?

"They said he came back from the dead."
   Nearly a whisper from behind me.
"Who said what?" I nearly shouted.
"Some saw him."
"Did you?" I did shout.
"No, but many did. He said he would."
I looked around, but the others paid no attention.
      As if not wanting to hear.

Hmm, that would make any place famous.

TWENTY THREE
The Sign

I finished the sign,
    and burned it.
Didn't seem right.
I didn't believe it would make a difference.
Could be trouble hanging a sign,
    "Yeshua Born Here."
I don't need trouble with Roman soldiers.
    And that is no way to remember my little
    friend.
What had gotten into me?
    This family—this child—was all I thought
    about. How could I think about not thinking
    about…?

I told all at my bar who would listen about the boy
    born in my barn.
The little boy with ancient eyes.
I showed them the manger,

that I had placed in a place of honor.
I pointed to the board with the drawing,
     now faded.
I pointed to the olive tree he drew for me, the symbol
     of God's convenant.
I told them about the kings that came.
     I told them that he was a miracle.
But I didn't talk about the slaughter;
     old nightmares and sleepless nights.

But I could talk about the parchment. I could show
     them the writing Jared gave me to keep.
          The writing the rabbis won't discuss.

"Hadad, you must stop telling all those dumb stories
     about Yeshua. You are running off all your
     customers." Guess who? Beatrice.

"I can't, Beatrice. I told you. I can't"

     And I didn't.

TWENTY FOUR
The Goodbye

But let me tell you what I did do.

"Jared, we should go to Bethany and see about
    Lazarus."
"Hadad, what about your business?"
"We should go to Jerusalem and talk to any
    eyewitnesses."
"What will you do about the inn?"
"We should see the tomb where they laid Yeshua
    and if he is still there."
"What will you do for money?"
"We might need to go to Nazareth and look for
    Mary and Joseph."
"What will you tell Beatrice?"

"Look, I'll not hang round here and do nothing. I've
    done that long enough. I'm not going to won-
    der for the rest of my life about the baby, this

man, all the stories. There is too much at stake. You met them. You knew there was something exceptional about all of them. What about the kings that came? What about the miracle when they escaped the slaughter? Jared, think about that. All of Rome sent to kill just one. It took them thirty years. And now so many say he's still alive. This is a chance of a lifetime. The question of a lifetime. Is he alive? Is he the blessed one? Had God come to town? Have you thought about the fact that the census brought them here in the first place? And, Jared, what about the miracles. All those that stopped at the bar and told us of miracles—the blind receive their sight, the lame walk, leprosy is cured, the deaf can hear again, even the dead are raised—Jared this is good news."

"Who will tend your bar?"

"Jared, you're my best friend, you will tend the bar until I return, if I return."

"If?"

"Just wait, let me finish before I change my mind. As far as the business, it's yours. The inn, the bar, the stable, the everything."

"Everything?"

"Yes, call it a partnership. Yours, to do with as you will."

"And, Beatrice?"

"She will go with me, of course."

"Does she know that?"

"Not yet, but she will."

"Hadad, are you sure? Beatrice will just pick up and leave? You trust me with everything? What about...? You are acting...different, changed"

"That's it exactly, Jared. Exactly. I'm different, changed. Yes, thank you for saying so. I knew there was something different, and it's me. Hah! So simple, it's me that's different. Who wouldn't be? And Beatrice understands. Things are different, hah, there it is again, *different*, things are different between us, like brand new again."

"But, just up and leaving?
Leaving everything behind?"

"Jared, I'm not leaving anything compared to what I'm gaining. Should a man not leave all he has to gain all he doesn't have? Should I die not knowing?"

"You are scarring me, Hadad."

"Oh, Jared, my friend, so many times I'd wish I had gone to see for myself. To Bethany. To Jerusalem. To speak with Bozra. Each time someone or something stopped me. Not now. This family, this boy, this Yeshua taught me for the first time what it feels like to think of someone but myself. That's a miracle to me. Jared, I... I love you. Did you hear me? I do. I love Beatrice. Haven't said that in years. I love Lydia too, and, well just about everybody."

"But...?"

"No buts. And, Jared, you must take care of Lydia. She needs a purpose for living. I know—give her a room and ask her to help you manage the place. That's it. Promise?"

"Yes. Of course. Whatever you say?"

"Good-bye my friend."

For additional copies of Mac's novels
please contact your local book store.

Also available:

www.BarnesAndNoble.com
www.Amazon.com
www.OneWayBooks.com

Bookstores please contact
STL Distribution
(800) 289-2772
www.STL-Distribution.com

All proceeds from book sales go to
One Way Books, a non-profit corporation.

ONE WAY BOOKS

For more information and book signing dates:
www.OneWayBookS.org
www.BibleActor.com
(954) 680-9095